This coloring
book belongs to:

Welcome!

Colouring is one of the most famous ways to decompress and reduce stress or anxiety. The colour palette you use while colouring helps you not only to calm and find inner peace, but also to tune with your creative self.

Enjoy 80 uniquely created ancient civilization designs in mandala style!

Happy Colouring,

Rebecca Green

THANK YOU VERY MUCH FOR PURCHASING THIS BOOK...

.... because **YOU** give colours to this world and our book.

Positive feedback from you really helps us to improve our work and deliver the best content. We would deeply appreciate if you wouldn't mind leaving an online review section.

Rebecca Green

Rebecca Green